Hello, Family Members,

D0660171

Learning to read is one of the most impor
of early childhood. **Hello Reader!** books
children become skilled readers who lil
readers learn to read by remembering f
like "the," "is," and "and"; by using phonics skills to decode new words; and by interpreting picture and text clues. These books provide both the stories children enjoy and the structure they need to read fluently and independently. Here are suggestions for helping your child *before*, *during*, and *after* reading:

Before

- Look at the cover and pictures and have your child predict what the story is about.
- Read the story to your child.
- Encourage your child to chime in with familiar words and phrases.
- Echo read with your child by reading a line first and having your child read it after you do.

During

- Have your child think about a word he or she does not recognize right away. Provide hints such as "Let's see if we know the sounds" and "Have we read other words like this one?"
- Encourage your child to use phonics skills to sound out new words.
- Provide the word for your child when more assistance is needed so that he or she does not struggle and the experience of reading with you is a positive one.
- Encourage your child to have fun by reading with a lot of expression . . . like an actor!

After

- Have your child keep lists of interesting and favorite words.
- Encourage your child to read the books over and over again. Have him or her read to brothers, sisters, grandparents, and even teddy bears. Repeated readings develop confidence in young readers.
- Talk about the stories. Ask and answer questions. Share ideas about the funniest and most interesting characters and events in the stories.

I do hope that you and your child enjoy this book.

—Francie Alexander
Reading Specialist,
Scholastic's Instructional Publishing Group

For Grace Maccarone
—B.L.

No part of this publication may be reproduced, or stored in a retrieval system, or transmitted in any form or by any means, electronic, mechanical, photocopying, recording, or otherwise, without written permission of the publisher. For information regarding permissions, write to Scholastic Inc., Attention: Permissions Department, 555 Broadway, New York, NY 10012.

Copyright © 1998 by Betsy Lewin.
All rights reserved. Published by Scholastic Inc.
SCHOLASTIC, HELLO READER! and CARTWHEEL BOOKS and associated logos are trademarks and/or registered trademarks of Scholastic Inc.

Library of Congress Cataloging-in-Publication Data

Lewin, Betsy.
Wiley learns to spell / by Betsy Lewin.
p. cm.—(Hello reader! Level 1)
"Cartwheel Books."
Summary: A mischievous monster named Wiley learns to spell.
ISBN 0-590-10835-2
[1. Monsters—Fiction. 2. English language—Spelling—Fiction.]
I. Title. II. Series.
PZ7.L58417We 1998
[E]—dc21 97-41142
CIP
AC

10 9 8 7 6 5 4 3 9/9 0/0 01 02

Printed in the U.S.A. 24
First printing, September 1998

WILEY LEARNS TO SPELL

by Betsy Lewin

Hello Reader! — Level 1

SCHOLASTIC INC.
Cartwheel BOOKS®
New York Toronto London Auckland Sydney

This is Wiley.
He can do anything.

What have you got there, Wiley?

V

The alphabet!
Can you spell CAT?

HIJKLM
NOPQRS

That is almost right,
Wiley.
Do you want to
try again?

HIJ LM
KAT

Not yet, Wiley.
Keep trying.

QAT
KAAT

That's right, Wiley.

CAT

You have eight letters,
Wiley.
Can you make a word
from them?

ELEPHANT

Unscramble the letters, Wiley.

LANT

Very good, Wiley!

ANT

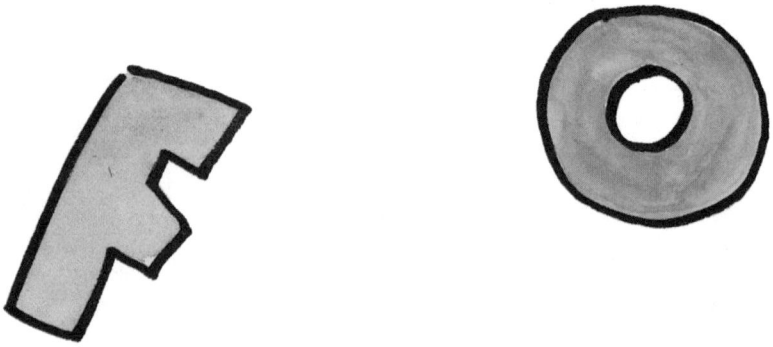

I think that you are
trying to tell me
something.
What could it be?

R
G

Frog!
Wiley, you are wonderful!

What do you plan to do
with these letters?

HSIMOP
TAPP

That is only part of a
word, Wiley.
Where is the other part?

POTA

Very funny, Wiley.
You made a spelling joke!
Now let's spell it right.

OSE

Thank you, Wiley!
You spell very well!